DINOSAUR FIGHTS

TYRANT VS. THREE-HORNED

BOOK 1: THE TYRANT

RAYMOND SHUMANSKY

Copyright © 2024 Raymond Shumansky

The moral right of the author has been asserted.

Apart from any fair dealing for the purposes of research or private study, or criticism or review, as permitted under the Copyright, Designs and Patents Act 1988, this publication may only be reproduced, stored or transmitted, in any form or by any means, with the prior permission in writing of the publishers, or in the case of reprographic reproduction in accordance with the terms of licences issued by the Copyright Licensing Agency. Enquiries concerning reproduction outside those terms should be sent to the publishers.

This is a work of fiction. Names, characters, businesses, places, events and incidents are either the products of the author's imagination or used in a fictitious manner. Any resemblance to actual persons, living or dead, or actual events is purely coincidental.

Troubador Publishing Ltd
Unit E2 Airfield Business Park,
Harrison Road, Market Harborough,
Leicestershire. LE16 7UL
Tel: 0116 2792299
Email: books@troubador.co.uk
Web: www.troubador.co.uk

ISBN 978 1805143 666

British Library Cataloguing in Publication Data.
A catalogue record for this book is available from the British Library.

Printed and bound in Great Britain by 4edge Limited
Typeset in 11pt Minion Pro by Troubador Publishing Ltd, Leicester, UK

'It's all in the jaws. This is the predator which had the strongest bite force of any terrestrial animal.'

– Raymond Shumansky

BACKGROUND

Scientists have invented a time machine. It was only the first one, though, so it could only send a single particle back in time. It was also limited to travelling to the past only, due to the fact that our future was not yet determined: matter sent forward in time would disintegrate as it is being divided between the infinite number of possible futures. So this breakthrough sparked little interest. That is, until the particles our soul is made up of have been discovered.

You see, as it turns out, the human soul had the natural ability to rearrange itself in order to rebuild its original shape and consciousness. This meant the existing time machine could simply send one's spirit back in time, particle by particle, into the body of a person or a creature, leaving its original body in a temporary comatose state until its return. We learnt that the body doesn't die without a soul, but rather, if the soul stays outside of any living body for too long, its body of origin dies. People started exploring the prehistoric world, looking through the eyes of the dinosaurs themselves. The past that is much closer to us (the history of our civilization), was a lot more difficult to research, because when two human souls were in the same body, they would simply fight for control over it endlessly. Primitive creatures, by contrast, could be fully subdued. The lower an animal's evolutionary complexity, the easier it was to control. Simpler life forms like insects, of course, were incompatible for soul transfer. It was both possible and very fun for us to experience and navigate the fight between any two dinosaurs. After this breakthrough, time machines were made illegal in order to preserve the state of our reality. A man named Jackson Tremblay has secretly built a soul time-portal in his basement and tonight he is going to test it with his friend Lucas Roy.

Jackson adjusted the two wooden chairs on each side of the table in the middle of the basement and the two men seated themselves. After a short discussion about the two dinosaurs which were going to clash in this duel, Jackson got off his chair, went to the corner, uncovered the soul time-portal and placed it in the middle of the table. The device resembled a folded, metallic umbrella. Jackson tweaked a few knobs at its top and then sat back in his chair opposite Lucas. The STP unfolded and began shooting rays from underneath. A second later, the two men passed out on the table.

65,805,293 YEARS AGO

Dark skies pierced by lightning strikes, scattered bones with decomposing flesh still attached to them, and the sight of vicious Tyrannosaurs. A whole pack of them. The largest is walking out of this lair of beasts. As he walks through the ash-covered ground, a raging volcano erupts in the distance, sending a barrage of fiery cinders raining down, randomly setting dead trees on fire. As the bristling Tyrant stomps ahead, his body brushes against a burning branch, inflaming his side. He continues without flinching, unconcerned with the flame that causes a mere sting, advancing ever so formidable, a true creature of hell himself.

At some distance from the Tyrant, a herd of horned dinosaurs is urgently striding away from the volcano. Suddenly the herd stops. An enormous Triceratops heads in the opposite direction. The mass of Three-horned dinosaurs splits apart, making way for him: a one-eyed male, covered in scars that tell of his past battles.

Another explosive eruption of the volcano shoots pieces of magma into the sky. One of the pieces hits a colossal pterosaur – Quetzalcoatlus – and his burning body starts descending to the ground. The falling giant is an omen of a gathering storm.

The Tyrant approaches and so does the Three-horned. A few small ornithopods from the species of Thescelosaurus cross the path of the predator whilst running away from the wrath of nature. The Tyrant snatches away one of them with his teeth, then crushes its body, spilling blood in all directions. As he continues on his path, the smoke coming from his side gradually diminishes.

The two dinosaurs carrying souls of men finally reach each other. They will fight to the death, but you will not read about their battle. Instead, you and your friend will each choose a prehistoric species and use this double gamebook as a soul time-portal. Welcome to the brutal world of dinosaurs!

INTRODUCTION

If you would like to read this gamebook on your own, simply begin by reading section 1 on page 17.

If you would like to try a two-player game, you need to have *Book 2: The Three-horned*, and begin reading the Two-Player Instructions on page 1.

If you would like to try the different move sequences used in two-player games on your own, and you do not have *Book 2: The Three-horned*, begin reading the Player vs. Automa (a simulated opponent) Instructions on page 5.

TWO-PLAYER INSTRUCTIONS

SET UP

* Before you start, you are going to need two pieces of paper, a pen or pencil, and a friend.
* Each of you chooses the Tyrant or Three-horned book, depending on which dinosaur you would like to be in this fight.
* There are Attack sheets which describe your attacks/moves. They are on pages 9 to 16. You can cut these pages out if you would like to use them for quick reference.
* Read the description of the attacks (on the sheets) of the dinosaur you chose in order to familiarise yourself with them.
* You are advised to copy the Two-Player Game Journal on page 4 on a separate piece of paper and place it between you and your opponent so both of you can always have an up to date record of the fight.

PLAYING THE GAME

STARTING: The two players start by reading section 2 (on page 17) in their respective books. Throughout the game, both of you should read the same section at the same time and wait for each other to finish. This is because the same section in both books represents a given situation viewed from two different perspectives.

ROUND SEQUENCE: The fight is divided into rounds. Each round:

1. You choose one attack.
2. Write the part of its name that is underlined on a piece of paper and place it face down. Make sure the other player does not see what you have written.
3. Both players reveal their attacks by flipping their pieces of paper. There are instructions in *Italics* on which section to read next.
4. The section which follows will describe the outcome in this round and give you further directions.
5. After the round ends, write down the attack names and remaining hit points in the Game Journal.

* Follow all instructions given in *Italics* and write down any code words at the bottom of the Game Journal.
* Both dinosaurs have 5 hit points.
* You win the game when your opponent runs out of hit points.
* Write "wait" instead of your attack's name to choose your attack after you have seen your opponent's. This way, you can choose a move which counters theirs. You can do this up to two times per fight and it can be done twice in the same round. If both dinosaurs wait this wastes one "wait" per player, after which both of you should go back to choosing your attack whilst still being in the same round.

EXAMPLE: You choose to wait in the first round and your attack counters that of your opponent. In the second round both of you choose to wait at first, so you both use this ability to no benefit. The second round then depends on the attacks you choose after the initial waiting. In the third round your enemy uses his last "wait", which allows him to counter you and win the round.

* Add a "–" after the name of your attack to use "speed". Any attack executed with speed automatically wins (even if the opponent was "waiting") and the two players need to read the first paragraph of the sheet which describes the attack instead of any section in the books. You then go to section 8. "Speed" can be used only once per battle. If both players use their "speed" at the same time, they would have to read the section in their books which describes the outcome in this round as usual.
* After one fight, you may choose to switch books for a fair rematch. If both of you get one victory each, to determine who won overall, simply compare who had more hit points when they won a fight.

> Tip: You can use dinosaur figures to help you understand the fight better.

TWO-PLAYER GAME JOURNAL

Round	Tyrant		Three-horned
	Attacks	Remaining Hit Points After The Round	Attacks
1			
2			
3			
4			
5			
6			
7			
Code words:			

PLAYER VS. AUTOMA INSTRUCTIONS

SET UP

* Before you start, you are going to need a piece of paper and pen or, preferably, a pencil.
* There are Attack sheets which describe your attacks/moves. They are on pages 9 to 16. You can cut these pages out if you would like to use them for quick reference.
* Read the description of the attacks (on the sheets) in order to familiarise yourself with them.
* There are two modes for the Automa (the simulated opponent) – Focused and Berserker. A Focused Automa mostly uses attacks which deal less damage but have a higher rate of success. The Berserker is programmed to do the opposite – it attempts to deal as much damage as possible irregardless of using attacks with a lesser success rate.
* After you choose whether you would like to go against the Focused or Berserker Automa, you are advised to copy its respective Game Journal on a separate piece of paper or use a pencil when making entries. The Automa Game Journals are on pages 7 and 8.

PLAYING THE GAME

STARTING: You begin the game by reading section 8.

ROUND SEQUENCE: The fight is divided into rounds. Each round:

1. You choose one attack.
2. Write the part of its name that is underlined in the Game Journal.
3. The same Game Journal will tell you which section reveals your opponent's chosen attack for this round. You should write its name in the journal as well.
4. After this, you should read the instructions in *Italics* in section 8 to see which section comes next.
5. The section that follows will describe the outcome in this round and give you further directions.

> IMPORTANT! Sections 4 and 7 are Two-Player only! When asked to go there you should go back to section 8 instead.

6. After the round ends, write down the remaining hit points in the Game Journal.

* Follow the instructions given in *Italics* and write down any code words at the bottom of the Game Journal.
* Both dinosaurs have 5 hit points.
* You win the game when your opponent runs out of hit points.

> Tip: You can use dinosaur figures to help you understand the fight better.

PLAYER VS. AUTOMA GAME JOURNAL

FOCUSED MODE

Round	Tyrant		Three-horned	
	Attacks	Remaining Hit Points After The Round	Attacks	Attack revealed in sec.
1				3
2				16
3				29
4				5
5				19
6				12
7				21
Code words:				

PLAYER VS. AUTOMA GAME JOURNAL

BERSERKER MODE

Round	Tyrant		Three-horned	
	Attacks	Remaining Hit Points After The Round	Attacks	Attack revealed in sec.
1				32
2				43
3				50
4				36
5				47
6				39
Code words:				

TOP ATTACK

First, you step on the head of the Three-horned in order to immobilise his greatest weapon – the forward-facing horns. You place your sole on the side of his head in order to avoid damage by the spikes. Next, you bite the side of your opponent's back, dealing 2 points of damage.

This attack is often successful because you're taller than the herbivorous dinosaur and that makes it easier to attack him from the top. The flaw of this sequence is that you could end up in a dangerous position if you don't neutralise your opponent's horns properly.

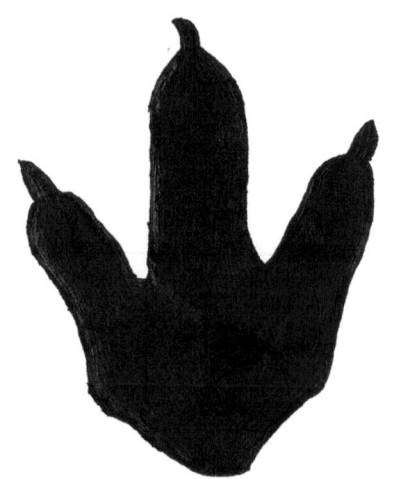

KICK

First, you step back with your left foot to create the necessary support, then you kick the head of the herbivorous dinosaur with your right foot, dealing 2 points of damage.

The skull of the Three-horned is wide, and the bony frill which protects his neck is an easy target. Because you're attacking from the side, you'll avoid the forward-facing horns of the enemy. The flaw of this move is that you'd leave your body position open, and if the Three-horned gets closer, he may land his blow successfully.

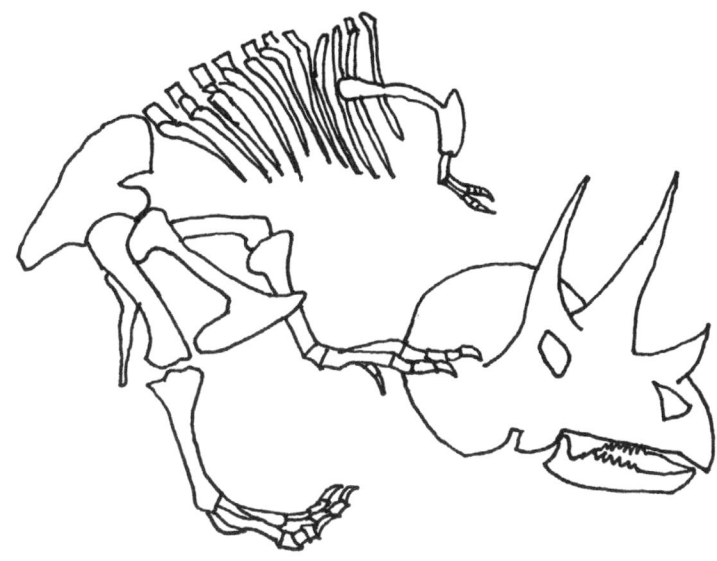

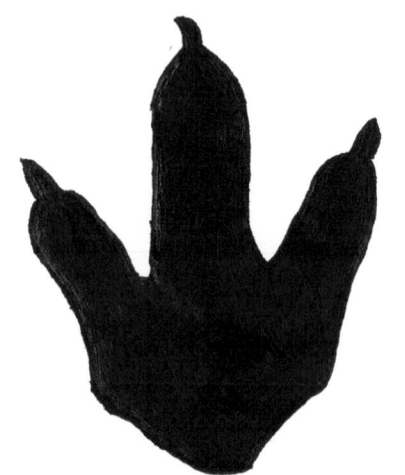

LOW ATTACK

You lower your body, tilting your head to the left, and then you bite the throat of the Three-horned, dealing 3 points of damage.

In this way you use your strongest weapon on his weakest point. The flaw of this move is that it can be difficult to reach below the beak of your opponent, and your lowered position makes you vulnerable to a variety of attacks.

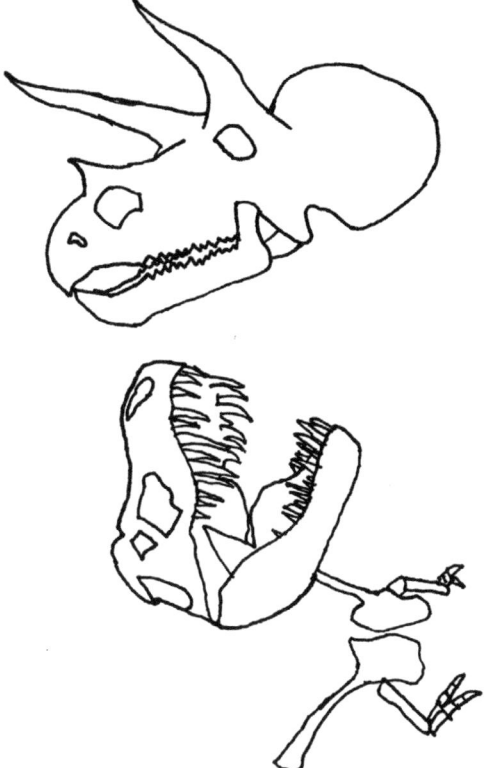

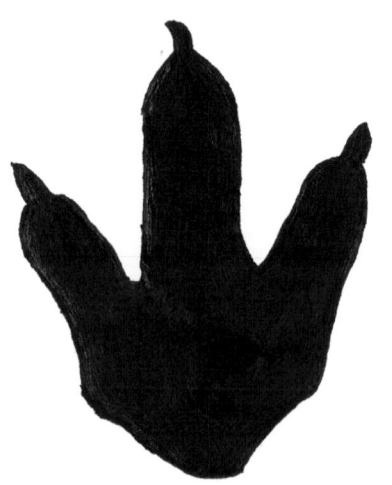

TAIL STRIKE

As your tail points backwards, you have to rotate your body to the left first; then strike the Three-horned dinosaur's flank with it, dealing 1 point of damage.

By rotating your body, you actually move your torso away from the enemy, making it easy to evade their attack. The tail strike that follows is the perfect counter-attack. The only flaw of this move is that it deals little damage.

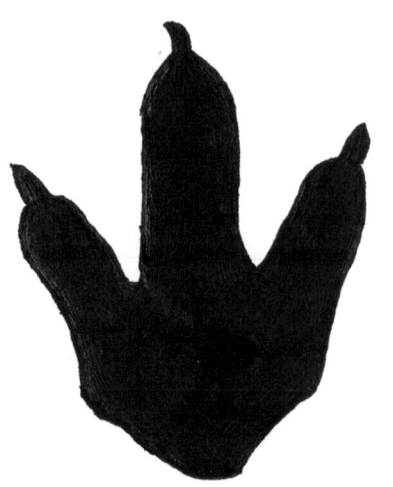

- 1 -

Your blood thirst and viciousness push you to attack the Three-horned dinosaur immediately. How will you do that? Will you try to attack him from the side, positioning yourself in his blind spot? Or will you use your strong leg to force his heavily armored head to turn away, following up with biting his back? Choose now!

Attack from the side – go to section 6.
Push his head away and bite his back – read section 9 next.

- 2 -

You begin to circle around the enemy in an attempt to position yourself in his blind spot to his left. The Three-horned, however, simply rotates his body to make sure you remain in his visual field. No more games! Time to strike!

The first two attacks available to you enable you to deal a good amount of damage without exposing yourself too much.

The moves available to you in this round are: Top attack and Kick. Read their description on your attack sheets (pages 9 to 12) and choose one. Write the name of your chosen attack on a piece of paper (making sure your opponent doesn't see what you wrote), then place it in front of you facing down. Only after both you and the other player have done this, you can continue reading the next instructions in *Italics*.

If you chose <u>Top</u> and your opponent has chosen <u>Roll</u>, go to section 11.

If your selected move is <u>Top</u> and the Three-horned's choice is <u>Push</u>, go to section 28.

If your chosen attack is <u>Kick</u> and your enemy has chosen <u>Roll</u>, go to section 17.

If you have chosen <u>Kick</u> and the other player chose <u>Push</u>, go to section 35.

— 3 —

The Tree-horned chose to <u>Kick</u> you in the first round.

Return to section 8.

— 4 —

You now have an advantage over your opponent thanks to the success of your initial attack. So, in this round you will have the option to drop all caution and go against your enemy with everything you've got. You now have all moves available to you: <u>Kick</u>, <u>Top</u> attack, <u>Low</u> attack and <u>Tail</u> strike.

Both you and your opponent should write the names of your attacks and reveal them, as instructed in the previous round. Only after both of you have done this, you can continue to the next instructions in *Italics*.

If the Three-horned has chosen <u>Horn</u> thrust as his move and yours is:

<u>Top</u> – *go to section 37.*
<u>Low</u> – *go to section 40.*
<u>Tail</u> – *go to section 42.*

<u>Kick</u> – go to section 44.
If the Three-horned has chosen a <u>Kick</u> to be his move and yours is:
   <u>Top</u> – go to section 20.
   <u>Low</u> – go to section 22.
   <u>Tail</u> – go to section 24.
   <u>Kick</u> – go to section 26.

– 5 –

In the fourth round, the Three-horned chooses <u>Push</u> as his move.

Return to section 8.

– 6 –

As you attempt to attack the Three-horned from the side, he simply turns to face you again and then counter-attacks by thrusting his horns towards the left side of your torso. The tips of his deadly protrusions begin to penetrate your skin. You start to feel sharp pain in your chest. You must react now! How will you respond to the opponent's bold move? Will you kick him in the head to stun him and stop him from inflicting further damage? Or will you use your tail to strike the side of his body to the same effect?

   Kick him in the head – go to section 10.
   Strike his side with your tail – go to section 14.

- 7 -

As you've just taken a blow, you're now at a disadvantage. It's time for a change in tactics, so you'll have a different set of attacks available to you. The moves available to you in this round are: Low attack and Tail strike.

Both you and your opponent should write the names of your attacks and reveal them, as instructed in the previous round. Only after both of you have done this, you can continue to the next instructions in *Italics*.

If your choice is the Low attack, and your opponent has chosen:
  Roll – go to section 13.
  Kick – go to section 22.
  Push – go to section 31.
  Horn – go to section 40.

If you chose the Tail strike, and the Three-horned has selected:
  Roll – go to section 15.
  Kick – go to section 24.
  Push – go to section 33.
  Horn – go to section 42.

- 8 -

Both players now have access to all their attacks.

After you and your opponent are ready with your choices and reveal them, you can check which section to read next as follows:

If you have chosen the Top attack as your move and the Three-horned's choice is:
    Roll – go to section 11.
    Kick – go to section 20.
    Push – go to section 28.
    Horn thrust – go to section 37.

If you chose the Low attack and the enemy has selected:
    Roll – go to section 13.
    Kick – go to section 22.
    Push – go to section 31.
    Horn thrust – go to section 40.

If your choice is Tail strike and your opponent has chosen:
    Roll – go to section 15.
    Kick – go to section 24.
    Push – go to section 33.
    Horn thrust – go to section 42.

If you decided your move is going to be the Kick and your adversary chose:
    Roll – go to section 17.
    Kick – go to section 26.
    Push – go to section 35.
    Horn thrust – go to section 44.

– 9 –

You place the sole of your foot on the side of the Three-horned's face and push his head out of the way. Then you bite his back. His scaly skin now presses against your gums, his back quills being your view as you taste his blood. Will you continue holding the herbivore with your jaws or will you kick his head to prevent him from resisting?

> *Continue tightening the bite – on section 18.*
> *Kick him in the head – on section 23.*

– 10 –

You lift your foot to kick the Three-horned in the head, but doing so causes you to lose balance and fall over as the other dinosaur keeps pushing you with his horns. You feel the spikes of the herbivore being pulled out of your chest as the enemy takes a step back before their final charge. Suddenly, as you lay on the ground, they thrust their protrusions through your gut. The sharp pain has you in agony. It's getting dark.

THE END

– 11 –

The Three-horned turns the right side of his body towards you while getting closer. But then you step on his face and bite his back. You feel your teeth sink into his flesh. Your enemy loses 2 hit points. After your attack, he pulls himself away from you and then both of you return to your initial stances.

> *Remember to write down the attack names and remaining hit points in the Game Journal! After this, go to section 4 unless you've already passed Round Two. If you have, go to section 8 instead.*

– 12 –

In the sixth round, the herbivore has decided to use his *Roll* move.

Return to section 8.

– 13 –

You lower your head in an attempt to bite the throat of your enemy, but he evades you by rotating his body to the left, thus moving his weak spot away from your jaws. While you're lowered like that, the Three-horned drops his body on top of yours, his left side pressing your head. You lose 2 hit points. The herbivorous dinosaur rolls his back over your spine, then lands on his feet. You get up and move away immediately. In this way, the two of you have returned to your initial positions.

Go/return to section 8.

– 14 –

Your powerful tail collides with the enemy's side with a thud. You pull yourself away from the horns of the other dinosaur. He is momentarily stunned and as you are very close to him, this is your perfect opportunity for a counter-attack. What will your move be? Will you bite the bony frill of the Three-horned in order to immobilise his greatest weapon? Or will you kick him in the head in order to continue with attacks which limit his focus?

Bite his frill – on section 25.
Kick him in the head – continue to section 27.

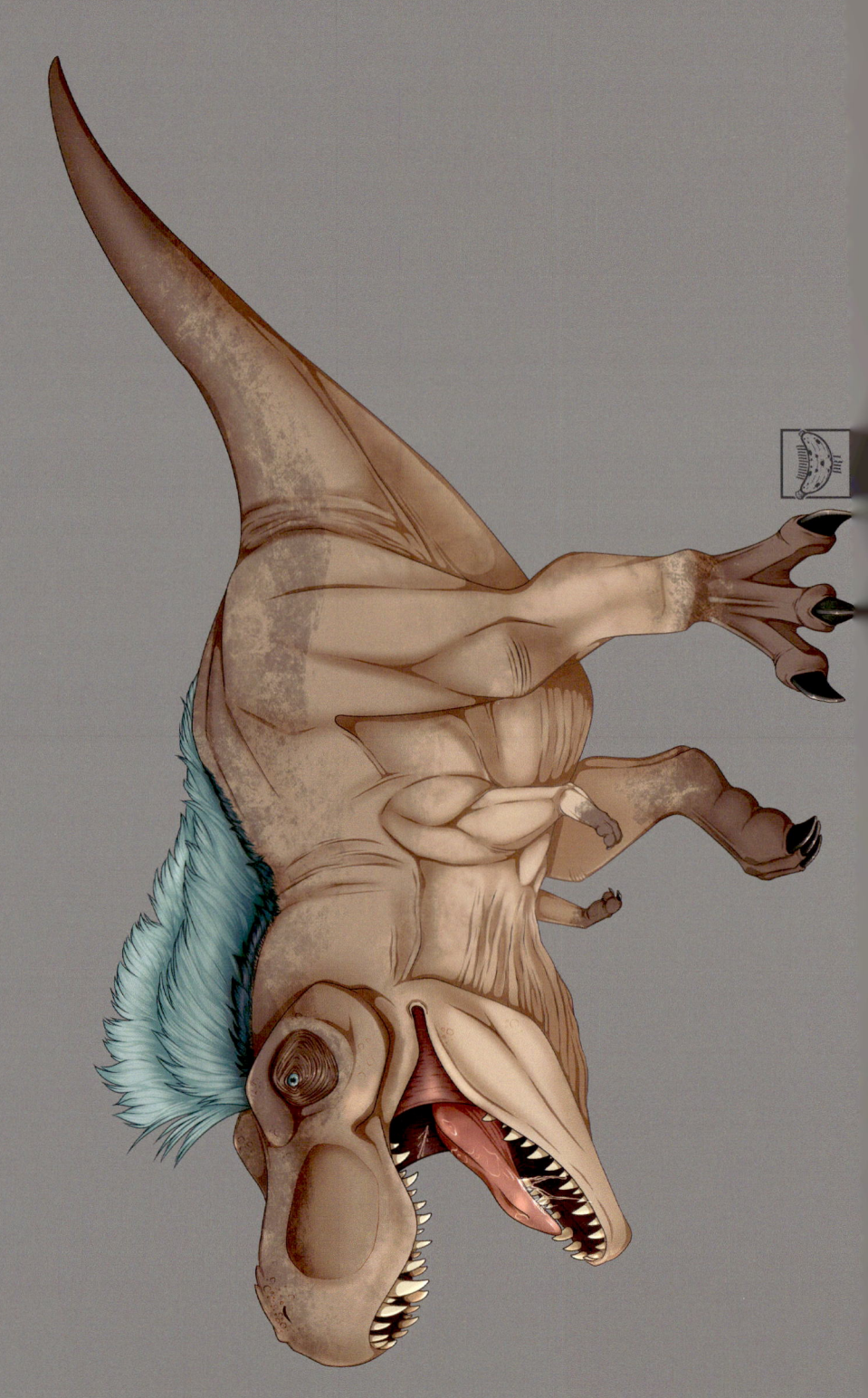

Art by Tarnah Inguanez

– 15 –

(If you have the code word "Injured" written, then read section 48 instead of this one.)

You rotate your body to the right. The Three-horned also turns his side towards you but you strike him with your tail before he could do anything. He loses 1 hit point. The herbivore takes a few steps back and the two of you return to your initial stances.

> You or your opponent should write down the code word "Bruised". If you already have that code word, write "Injured" instead. After this, you should go to section 8.

– 16 –

In the second round, the herbivore follows with a <u>Roll</u> move.

> Return to section 8.

– 17 –

You take a step back with your left foot, then you push it against the ground to spring forth. The Three-horned turns his right side towards you and starts moving closer. When you lift your right foot getting ready to kick him, he knocks your body down with his side, falling on top of you in the process. You begin to suffocate while feeling your ribs fracturing at the same time. This costs you 2 hit points. Your opponent gets his body off of you and moves away. You rise to your feet, and the two of you assume your initial positions facing each other.

Remember to write down the attack names and remaining hit points in the Game Journal! After this, go to section 7 unless you've already passed Round Two. If you have, go to section 8 instead.

– 18 –

As you continue your lock the enemy uses the side of their head to hit yours and force you to let them go. You are now too close to the other dinosaur, though this could be turned into an advantage. What is your next move? Will you use the opportunity of being this close to bite one of the front legs of your opponent and pull it to the side in an effort to have him lose balance and fall? Or will you begin turning your body in order to create momentum for a tail strike?

Go for his legs – on section 30.
Strike with your tail – read section 34 next.

– 19 –

Your opponent has the <u>Horn</u> thrust as his chosen attack.

Return to section 8.

– 20 –

The Three-horned turns his right side towards you and lifts his hind leg, but you avoid the rear of his body as you're going for his head instead. You step on his face bypassing his horns, then you use your height advantage to bite his back. Your teeth sink so deep into the flesh of the herbivore, you feel your gums pressing against his scaly skin. Your enemy loses 2 hit points. After your attack, he pulls himself away and the two of you return to your initial positions.

Go/return to section 8.

– 21 –

In this final round, the Three-horned will use *Push*.

Return to section 8.

– 22 –

(If you have the code word "Wounded" written, then read section 46 instead of this one.)

You lower your head going for the throat of the Three-horned, but he evades your jaws by turning his head to the left while rotating his entire body sideways. You end up being too close to the enemy, which is all the more dangerous with your posture being lowered. The herbivorous dinosaur kicks you in the ribs with his hind leg. You lose 1 hit point. After taking a couple of steps back, you return to your initial position. The other dinosaur does the same.

You or your opponent should write down the code word "Impaired". If you already have that code word, write "Wounded" instead. After this, you should go to section 8.

– 23 –

You try to kick the head of the herbivore, but apparently he was moving it to try and reach you. One of his horns goes right through the sole of your foot. The sharp pain causes you to let go of the other dinosaur's back. Unable to place your injured foot on the ground you begin to lose balance. The Three-horned runs his spikes through your chest and pushes further until you fall. You feel your lungs filling up with your own blood.

THE END

– 24 –

(If you have the code word "Wounded" written, then read section 46 instead of this one.)

You rotate your entire body in order to point your tail towards the opponent. At the same time he also turns sideways, but then he suddenly kicks you in the knee with his hind foot. You lose balance and collapse to the ground. This strike costs you 1 hit point. You rise as the Three-horned turns forward.

> *You or your opponent should write down the code word "Impaired". If you already have that code word, write "Wounded" instead. After this, you should go to section 8.*

- 25 -

You bite the frill of the herbivore. He struggles to break free. At this point this turns into a game of strength and balance. What will you do next? Will you suddenly let go to surprise your opponent and headbutt him right after? Or will you kick him in the head to have him lose focus?

> *Let go of the frill and follow with a headbutt – on section 38.*
> *Kick him in the head – go to section 41.*

- 26 -

(If you have the code word "Wounded" written, then read section 46 instead of this one.)

You take a step back in order to build momentum for your attack. The Three-horned turns his body sideways. When you lunge at him, he lifts his hind leg and kicks you in the stomach, knocking the wind out of you. While striking you, the herbivore pushes himself off of you rolling over his back until he gets back to his feet. This, of course, causes no damage to your enemy. At the same time, the pain from the taken blow causes you to fall heavily. You lose 1 hit point. It's time to get to your feet!

> *You or your opponent should write down the code word "Impaired". If you already have that code word, write "Wounded" instead. After this, you should go to section 8.*

– 27 –

You try to kick the Three-horned in the face, but you fail to do so because he rears up on his hind legs, raising his head higher. From here he knocks you down with his front legs. After you fall, he stomps you with them, knocking the air out of you as you hear the sound of your ribs getting fractured. The sudden pain in your chest is unbearable, but something much worse is coming – the herbivore drives his spikes into your chest.

THE END

– 28 –

You lift your right foot with the intention of using it to hold the Three-horned's head away from you while you attack him from the top. He, however, rears up, making it impossible to reach his head or back. The next thing the herbivore does is to knock you down with his front limbs. Your body hits the ground with a thud. This causes intense internal pain. You also feel your skin bruise as it drags across the rough surface. You've lost 2 hit points.

Remember to write down the attack names and remaining hit points in the Game Journal! After this, go to section 7 unless you've already passed Round Two. If you have, go to section 8 instead.

– 29 –

The other dinosaur has decided to use his *Kick* again in the third round.

Return to section 8.

- 30 -

You bite the herbivore's left front leg and start pulling in an effort to have him topple over. As your position is close to the ground, the enemy can't reach you with their spikes so you're safe to perform this attack move. The Three-horned, however, uses his sharp beak to bite your face. It easily cuts through your flesh to reach your bone. The pain forces you to let go of the other dinosaur's leg. After pulling yourself away, you feel his horns being driven into your chest.

THE END

- 31 -

You lower your position in an attempt to reach the Three-horned's throat with your jaws. At the same time, the herbivore rises up on his rear legs and stomps your upper back with his front feet, knocking you down to the ground and pressing even more with his mass. You've hit your snout in the fall. It's difficult to breathe with all that weight applying pressure on your ribcage. You lose 2 hit points. After the attack, the other dinosaur moves away and you rise to your feet.

Go/return to section 8.

- 32 -

In this first round, the Three-horned will go for a *Horn* thrust.

Return to section 8.

- 33 -

(If you have the code word "Injured" written, then read section 48 instead of this one.)

You turn your body sideways in order to position your tail closer to the enemy. In the meantime, he rears up and attempts to knock you down with his front legs. By rotating your body, however, you evade the herbivore's attack because, in this way, you move your head and chest away from him. After this, you counter-attack by striking the other dinosaur with your tail. Your powerful appendage collides with his side producing a thudding sound as it shoves the Three-horned. He loses 1 hit point. The two of you move away and turn your weapons towards each other – teeth versus horns.

> *You or your opponent should write down the code word "Bruised". If you already have that code word, write "Injured" instead. After this, you should go to section 8.*

- 34 -

You rotate your body in order to execute a tail strike. Your powerful appendage collides with the side of the herbivore's face. The slapping sound is clear proof your move was a success. Small bruises on your tail are a price worth paying as the Three-horned is visibly stunned. But what will you do next? Will you simply reach down to bite his throat? Or will you use your head to try and knock him down before your final attack?

> *Bite his throat – go to section 45.*
> *Knock him down first – on section 49.*

– 35 –

You take a step back with your left foot and plant it firmly to get a better grip on the ground for your next move. The Three-horned rears up and thrusts his front limbs towards you but he misses as you're moving away. As the herbivore brings his position down, you lunge at him, striking the side of his head with your right foot while bypassing his horns. The plant eater's head bounces back from the force of your kick. He loses 2 hit points. You move away after your successful attack.

Remember to write down the attack names and remaining hit points in the Game Journal! After this, go to section 4 unless you've already passed Round Two. If you have, go to section 8 instead.

– 36 –

In the fourth round, the opponent has decided to use *Push*.

Return to section 8.

– 37 –

You fail to step on the face of the Three-horned because he rears up on his hind legs. Next, he uses them to thrust his body forward, piercing your chest with his greatest weapon. The two longer horns sink halfway in. You pull yourself away but it's too late. The wounds are deep and blood is now flowing. Your insides suddenly feel cold as your skin feels the warmth of your vital fluid. This blow costs you 3 hit points.

Go/return to section 8.

- 38 -

You suddenly open your jaws to the surprise of your opponent. As he was just pulling and shaking in order to break free, the unexpected release has him briefly lose his footing. You take advantage of that immediately – using all your strength you push the herbivore with your head until he falls rolling over his back. You sink your teeth into his exposed throat. His desperate cries merely remind you that a feast is coming.

YOU WIN!

- 39 -

In this final round, the Three-horned will attack you with his *Horn*s.

Return to section 8.

- 40 -

The Three-horned rears up, getting ready to attack. However, this exposes his weak spot – something you take immediate advantage of. You bite his throat, feeling your teeth sinking in until your gums press against his scaly skin. In a desperate attempt to break free, the herbivore presses your upper back with his front limbs. You loosen the grip and pull your jaws away, so as to avoid having your head crushed by his mass. The blood of your enemy stains the ground. He loses 3 hit points.

Go/return to section 8.

- 41 -

You lift your foot to kick the head of the Three-horned. A sudden sharp pain reminds you that your opponent has a powerful beak. The herbivore starts pulling your limb until you lose balance and fall, hitting the ground with a thud. Having tasted your blood, the other dinosaur now uses his beak again to bite your underside while his deadly horns sink into your flesh. Then he shakes his head, tearing your belly.

THE END

- 42 -

(If you have the code word "Injured" written, then read section 48 instead of this one.)

You turn sideways in order to move your tail closer to the enemy. At the same time, he rears up and lunges at you with his horns facing forward. By rotating your body, however, you move your front away from the deadly protrusions, and then you counter-attack by striking the Three-horned's side with your tail. The immense appendage slams into the ornithischian with such force, it shoves his body. He loses 1 hit point. Next, you turn your head towards him again.

> *You or your opponent should write down the code word "Bruised". If you already have that code word, write "Injured" instead. After this, you should go to section 8.*

– 43 –

The herbivore has chosen to attack you with his *Horn*s again in the second round.

Return to section 8

– 44 –

You take a step back in order to create the necessary support for your next strike. The Three-horned rears up on his hind legs and uses them to thrust his body forward with his horns pointed towards you. This, however, doesn't move his head away from the path of your foot, so you kick the side of his face as you bypass his horns with your sole. The ornitischian loses 2 hit points, his head bounced off badly.

Go/return to section 8.

– 45 –

You crouch in order to reach the throat of the Three-horned. He is unable to react quickly enough as you cut into his flesh with your teeth. Your bite is the strongest there ever was! The enemy collapses a few moments later. Their blood is flowing across your face.

YOU WIN!

- 46 -

As you begin to make your move, you suddenly stop. The Three-horned is starting to turn his body sideways and you've already seen what he'll do next. Using the same move over and over again may work in video games, but in a real situation the opponent would learn to counter it. Before the herbivorous dinosaur turns completely, you react by instinct and lunge towards his side, biting the upper part of his thigh so he wouldn't be able to lift his leg. Then, you tighten the grip of your jaws, feeling your teeth press against the thighbone of the other dinosaur while causing serious damage to tissue in the process. Your enemy loses 2 hit points.

Return to section 8.

- 47 -

The enemy chose *Roll* this round.

Return to section 8.

- 48 -

The Three-horned suddenly stops to observe as you begin to rotate your body. He's already seen what you'll do next. Using the same move over and over again may work in video games, but in a real situation the opponent would learn to counter it. The herbivore suddenly lunges at you, biting your leg just under the knee with his beak. He then starts shaking his head and as he moves, one of his longer horns cuts a wound in the lower part of your thigh. You manage to pull yourself away. It feels like your leg is getting wet. You look down to see that you're bleeding. Being predictable costs you 2 hit points.

Return to section 8.

– 49 –

You move forward rapidly to strike the side of the herbivore's body with your forehead. This ramming attack knocks him down successfully. You waste no time to close your jaws tightly with the throat of the Three-horned between them. He is now at your mercy, but you have none. You keep holding the other dinosaur. The metallic taste of his blood fills your senses. He finally stops moving.

YOU WIN!

– 50 –

In the third round, the other dinosaur is going for the *Horn* thrust again.

Return to section 8.

EPILOGUE

Jackson and Lucas opened their eyes and lifted their heads. After taking their hands out of the two openings on the side of the table, the two then proceeded to remove their cable-riddled helmets.

'Wait…' Lucas became serious all of a sudden. 'Just had a déjà vu. It felt as if we've done this exact fight, but we did it using an illegally built STP you had in your basement.'

'I've just had the same déjà vu,' said Jackson. 'We weren't at this military base.'

'What do you think this means?' asked Lucas…

THE TEN MOST BRUTAL AND FASCINATING DINOSAUR FIGHTS

Tyrannosaurus vs. Triceratops

Spinosaurus vs. Carcharodontosaurus

Therizinosaurus vs. Tarbosaurus

Stegosaurus vs. Allosaurus

Utahraptor vs. Gastonia

Tyrannosaurus vs. Ankylosaurus

Velociraptor vs. Protoceratops

Pachycephalosaurus vs. Dromaeosaurus

Herrerasaurus vs. Saurosuchus

Shunosaurus vs. Sinraptor